THIS BLOOMSBURY BOOK

BELONGS TO

....

Can't Sleep Without Sheep

Susanna Leonard Hill   illustrated by **Mike Wohnoutka**

BLOOMSBURY

LONDON   BERLIN   NEW YORK

Bloomsbury Publishing, London, Berlin and New York

First published in Great Britain in March 2011 by Bloomsbury Publishing Plc
36 Soho Square, London, W1D 3QY

First published in the USA in September 2010 by Walker Publishing Company Inc
175 Fifth Avenue, New York, NY 10010

Text copyright © Susanna Leonard Hill 2010
Illustrations copyright © Mike Wohnoutka 2010
The moral right of the author and illustrator has been asserted

A CIP catalogue record of this book is available from the British Library

ISBN 978 1 4088 1392 8

All papers used by Bloomsbury Publishing are natural, recyclable products made
from wood grown in well-managed forests. The manufacturing processes conform
to the environmental regulations of the country of origin

Printed in China by Hung Hing Printing (China) Co Ltd, Shenzhen, Guangdong

1 3 5 7 9 10 8 6 4 2

www.bloomsbury.com

For Eric, with love
S. L. H.

To Franklin and Olivia, sweet dreams
M. W.

Ava had a hard time falling asleep.
Her mind was always so busy!

'Try counting sheep,' suggested her mother.
So she did.

'One sheep jumping over the fence . . . two sheep jumping over
the fence . . . three sheep jumping over the fence . . .'

But her mind was full of ideas and questions, thoughts of today,
and plans for tomorrow.

Night after night, the sheep had to jump the fence *many* times.

'Can we *please* stop?' asked the sheep. 'We're exhausted.'

'No! I need you to keep jumping!' said Ava.

'In that case,' said the sheep, 'we quit.'

'You can't quit!' said Ava. 'How will I get to sleep?'

'Don't worry. We'll find a replacement,' they promised.

Horses seemed like the best choice. But they were so beautiful that Ava made the fence higher and wider to see how well they could jump.

'Horses are too much fun!' said the sheep. 'We need somebody less pretty. Send in the chickens.'

The chickens *tried* to get over the fence.

They *wanted* to get over the fence.

Ava laughed and laughed, but she did not go to sleep.

'We need somebody less ridiculous,' said the sheep. 'Pigs?'

The pigs were not in any hurry.
'One pig over the fence,' said Ava. Then she had
to wait while the others stopped to snack.
'Pigs are too slow,' decided the sheep.

The cows were a complete disaster!

This was harder than the sheep thought!
But they were just getting started.

The penguins looked at the fence, then looked at themselves.

'We need a plan,' they said.

'Next!' said the sheep.

The hippos waddled forward.
'This could take a while,' said one sheep.

The animals grew impatient.
'Is it our turn?' asked the herd of buffalo.
'No, *we're* next!' shouted the flamingos,
the armadillos and the beavers.
'We'll see about that!' roared the buffalo.

The stampede began as the buffalo charged
the fence.
   Dust rose in clouds. Splinters flew everywhere.
It was chaos!

'STOP!' cried Ava. 'I'll never get to sleep like this!'

'Wow,' said the sheep. 'Who knew we'd be so hard to replace?'
'I knew,' Ava replied. 'You always show up for work. You line
up nicely and jump calmly. You're fluffy and peaceful and perfect!'

'Well,' said one sheep. 'It's nice to be appreciated.'
'Please, will you stay?' begged Ava. 'I need you to help me fall asleep.'
'Don't worry,' said the sheep. 'You can count on us!'

So she did.